Tadpoles

# Pirate
# Pete

First published in 2007 by
Franklin Watts
338 Euston Road
London
NW1 3BH

Franklin Watts Australia
Level 17/207 Kent Street
Sydney
NSW 2000

A CIP catalogue record for this book is available
from the British Library.

ISBN 978 0 7496 7160 0 (hbk)
ISBN 978 0 7496 7304 8 (pbk)

**Series Editor:** Jackie Hamley
**Editor:** Melanie Palmer
**Series Advisor:** Dr Hilary Minns
**Series Designer:** Peter Scoulding

Printed in China

Franklin Watts is a division of
Hachette Children's Books.

# Pirate Pete

by Lynne Benton

## Illustrated by Neil Chapman

W

FRANKLIN WATTS
LONDON•SYDNEY

## Lynne Benton

"Q: What is green, has two legs and a chest?

A: A seasick pirate!"

## Neil Chapman

"When I was a boy, I liked to read about dragons, goblins and pirates. Now it is fun to draw them for my own children to see."

# Pete was a pirate.

One day he got
a letter.

It was a map of
a treasure island.

"I must find the treasure!" Pete said.

# He sailed to the island.

# He climbed up the hill.

He found a treasure chest ... and opened it.

"Oh!" said Pirate Pete.

16

Pirate Pete was
very surprised.

# They all had
# a great party.

"That was even more fun than finding treasure," said Pete.

# Notes for adults

**TADPOLES** are structured to provide support for newly independent readers. The stories may also be used by adults for sharing with young children.

Starting to read alone can be daunting. **TADPOLES** help by providing visual support and repeating words and phrases. These books will both develop confidence and encourage reading and rereading for pleasure.

**If you are reading this book with a child, here are a few suggestions:**

1. Make reading fun! Choose a time to read when you and the child are relaxed and have time to share the story.
2. Talk about the story before you start reading. Look at the cover and the blurb. What might the story be about? Why might the child like it?
3. Encourage the child to reread the story, and to retell the story in their own words, using the illustrations to remind them what has happened.
4. Discuss the story and see if the child can relate it to their own experience, or perhaps compare it to another story they know.
5. Give praise! Remember that small mistakes need not always be corrected.

## If you enjoyed this book, why not try another TADPOLES story?

**Sammy's Secret**
978 0 7496 6890 7

**Stroppy Poppy**
978 0 7496 6893 8

**I'm Taller Than You!**
978 0 7496 6894 5

**Leo's New Pet**
978 0 7496 6891 4

**Mop Top**
978 0 7946 6895 2

**Charlie and the Castle**
978 0 7496 6896 9

**Over the Moon!**
978 0 7496 6897 6

**My Sister is a Witch!**
978 0 7496 6898 3

**Five Teddy Bears**
978 0 7496 7292 8

**Little Troll**
978 0 7496 7293 5

**The Sad Princess**
978 0 7496 7294 2

**Runny Honey**
978 0 7496 7295 9

**Dog Knows Best**
978 0 7496 7297 3

**Sam's Sunflower**
978 0 7496 7298 0